GOOD NIGHT, GORILLA

Peggy Rathmann

G. P. Putnam's Sons

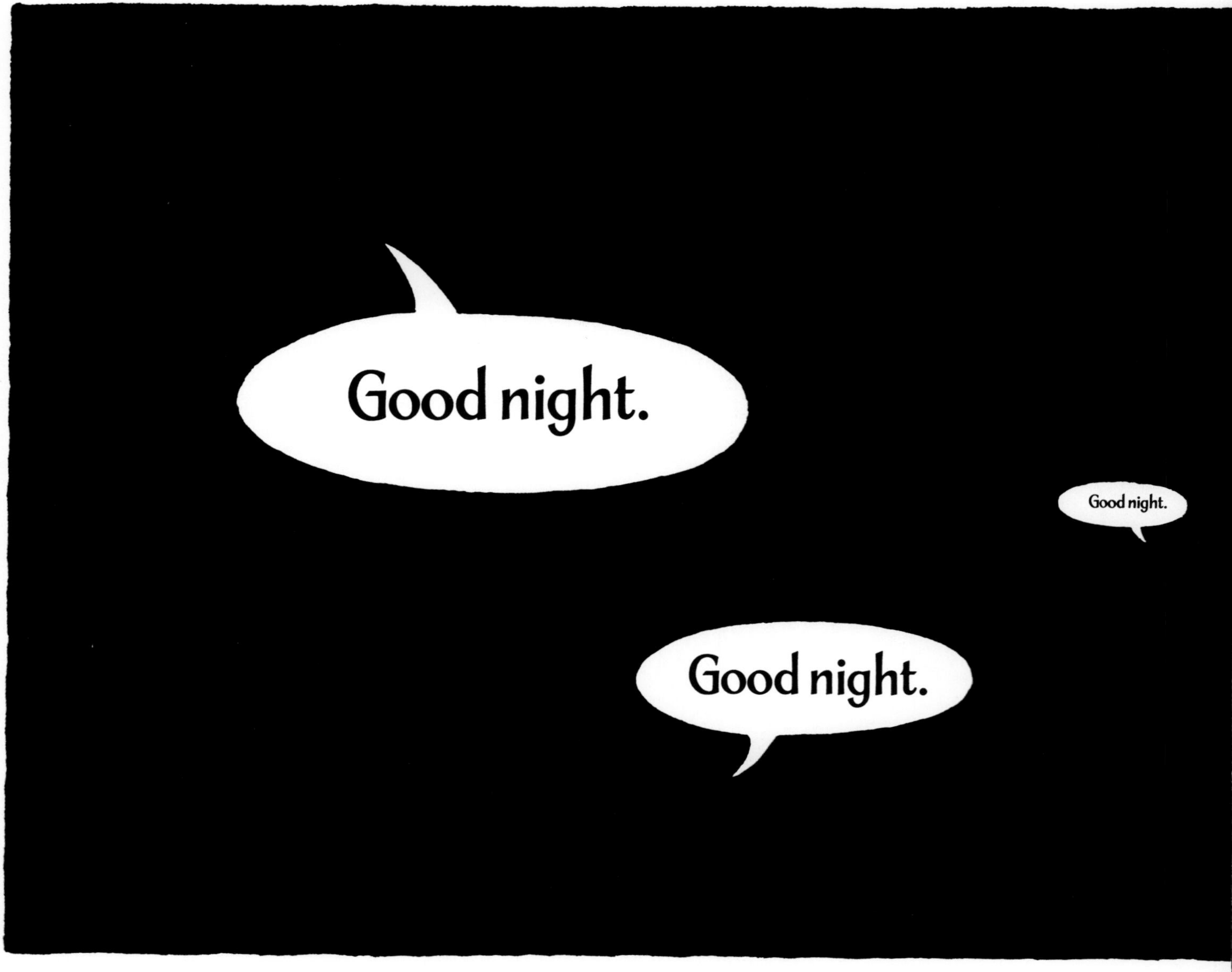
Good night.
Good night.
Good night.

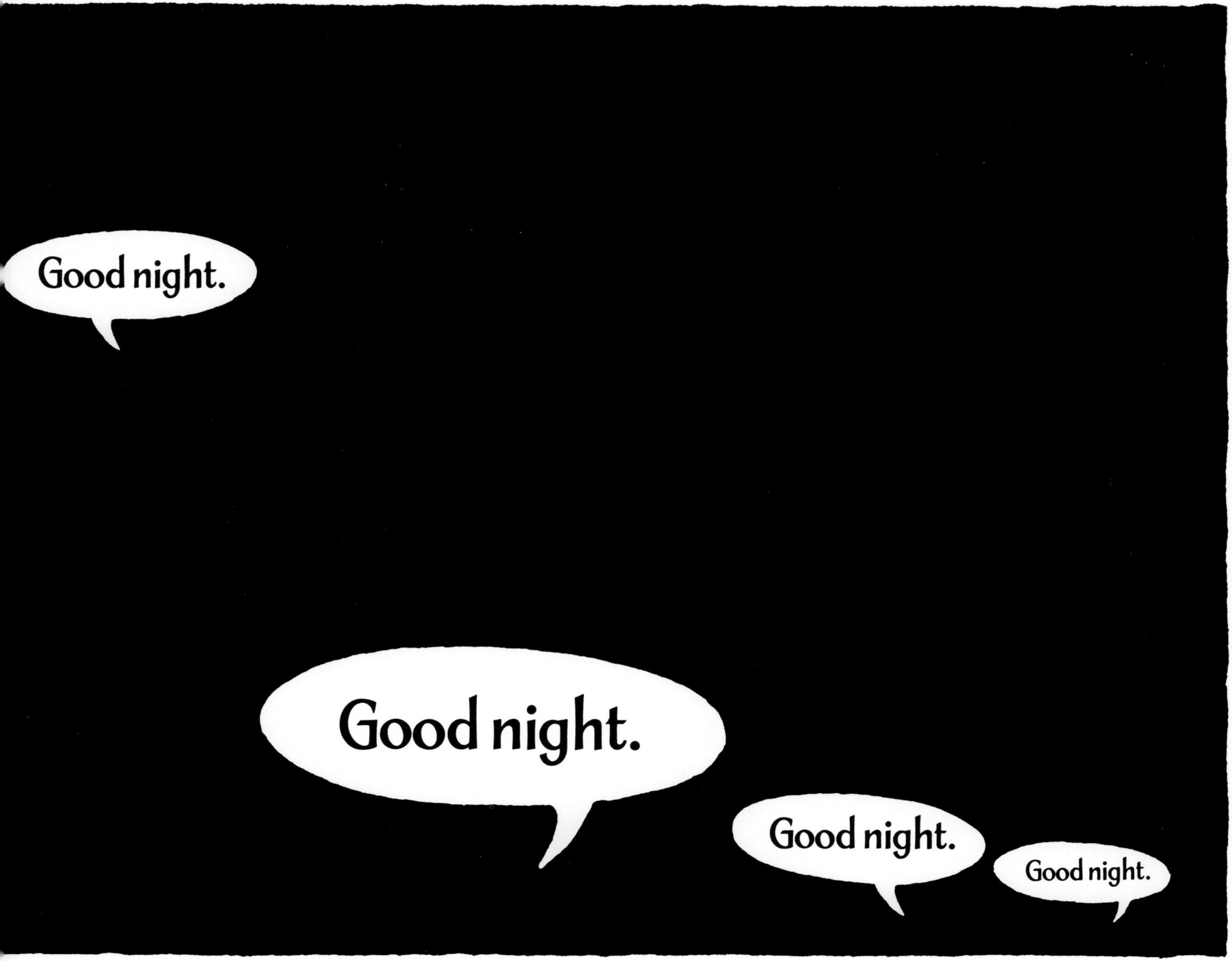
Good night.
Good night.
Good night.
Good night.

For Mr. and Mrs. Joseph McQuaid,
and all their little gorillas

Library of Congress Cataloging-in-Publication Data
Rathmann, Peggy. Good night, Gorilla / Peggy Rathmann. p. cm.
Summary: An unobservant zookeeper is followed home by
all the animals he thinks he has left behind in the zoo.
[1. Zoo animals—Fiction. 2. Zoos—Fiction.] I. Title. PZ7.R1936Go 1994
92-29020 CIP AC [E]--DC20
ISBN 0-399-22445-9
Special Markets ISBN 978-0-399-24700-2 Not for Resale
11 12 13 14 15 16 17 18 19 20

This Imagination Library edition is published by Penguin Young Readers, a division
of Penguin Random House, exclusively for Dolly Parton's Imagination Library,
a not-for-profit program designed to inspire a love of reading and learning, sponsored
in part by The Dollywood Foundation. Penguin's trade editions of this work are
available wherever books are sold.